Dinosaur's On The Prowl.

By

John C Burt.

1

This is the tale of : 'Dinosaur's On The Prowl?' You may never ..

ever, ever, thought of a Dinosaur as being an animal that can and does prowl around.

Pictured we have the very leader of the pack of Dinosaur's Robert or as..

7

he liked to be known Bob the Dinosaur with the Horns !!! There was a pesky volcano

that just, just,
kept
threatening
to erupt at
any given
minute or
second? Bob..

the Dinosaur
with Horns
was very
worried about
what this
volcano could
and would do?

Bob's friend Eddy the Green as green Dinosaur was worried as well? There

was a
Dinosaur egg
to be
considered as
well? What
would happen

to the young
as young and
not as yet
born
Dinosaur it
contained if

17

the local and near neighbor of a volcano went off? Paul the Horse Dinosaur was of the same mind as Bob and Eddy, he too was very, very , worried about the very volcano on their very doorstep and the Dinosaur egg and what would happen to it as well?

Bob, Eddy and the Paul the Horse Dinosaur could not help themselves ...

21

they went on
the Prowl
throughout
the very
Jungle's of
their area. A
bit like a Dad..

who is known to pace up and down before the birth of a child ?

23

24

The Mother Dinosaur Mildred the Purple Dinosaur was worried as well about ...

the coming eruption of the local volcano and her egg and what would happen to it?

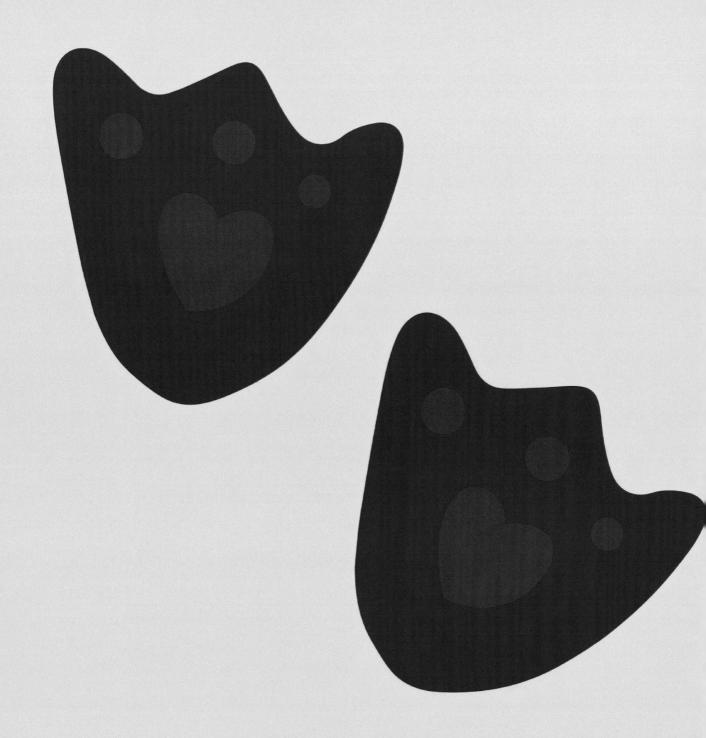

27

28

Mildred the Purple Dinosaur thought to herself she did not want ..

to be on the Prowl through the jungle like Bob, Eddy and Paul, she instead ......

would
maintain a
'stiff upper lip
in a crisis?'
She could not
see the point

in everybody
prowling,
prowling,
prowling
through the
jungle
worried as ..

worried about the volcano and it's chance of eruption? Mildred was..

sure as sure could be , that her egg and the three male Dinosaur's would live?

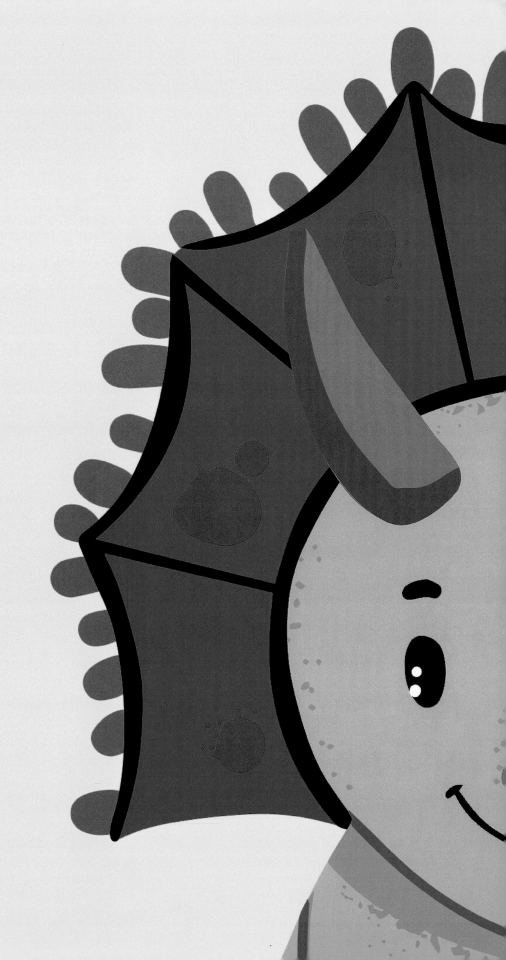

38

CPSIA information can be obtained
at www.ICGtesting.com
Printed in the USA
BVRC090958060721
611236BV00005B/43